DISCARD

PIERO VENTURA

# FOOD

**Its Evolution through the Ages**

With the Collaboration of

## Max Casalini

Marisa Murgo Ventura
Pierluigi Longo
Massimo Messina

Houghton Mifflin Company    Boston 1994

# CONTENTS

Copyright ©1994 by Arnoldo Mondadori Editore S.p.A.
English translation ©1994 by Arnoldo Mondadori Editore S.p.A.
First American edition 1994
Originally published in Italy in 1994 by Mondadori

All rights reserved. For information about permission to reproduce
selections from this book, write to Permissions, Houghton Mifflin Company,
215 Park Avenue South, New York, New York 10003.
   *Cataloging-in-Publication Data*

Ventura, Piero.
   (Cibi. English)
   Food: its evolution through the ages/Piero Ventura.—1st American ed.
   p.  cm.
   Translation of: I cibi
   ISBN 0-395-66790-9
   1. Food—History—Juvenile literature. 2. Food habits—History—
Juvenile literature. 3. Food supply—History—Juvenile literature.
(1. Food—history)    I. Title.
TX355.V4413   1994                              94-14419
641.3'09—dc20                                   CIP
                                                AC

Printed in Spain by Artes Gráficas Toledo, S.A.
10 9 8 7 6 5 4 3 2 1
D.L.TO:388-1994

# INTRODUCTION

The dictionary defines food as "material used in the body of an organism to sustain growth, repair, and vital processes and to furnish energy"—in other words, we need food to live and grow. The study of how people have responded to this natural need leads us back over the major steppingstones of history and human evolution.

How did people learn to hunt and fish? When did people change from being hunters and gatherers to farmers with domestic livestock? How did the ancient Egyptians and Romans get their food? How did the foods of the New World change people's eating habits? What effects do the foods we eat have on us? What advantages did steam power bring to agriculture? What is the history of food preservation? How have the sterilization and pasteurization of foods had a major role in stopping the spread of disease? Why is a balanced diet important to good health? How might genetic engineering resolve the problems of world hunger?

This book answers these and other questions as it traces the fascinating history of people and food.

## HUNTING WITH PITS AND SNARES

This story has its roots so deep in the distant past that it is difficult to imagine a time when man was the last to arrive on Earth and the real rulers of the prairies were the lions, hyenas, rhinoceros, buffalo, and the tusked and saber-toothed tigers. Thousands and thousands of years had to pass before this new species, man, began to get the upper hand over the animals and nature. This was determined by man's ability to make weapons and tools, which allowed him to confront and catch wild animals for food. The first preys of the early hunters were small animals that could be caught in traps and in holes dug in the ground or even chased from high crags so that they could then be captured and killed.

*To capture their prey, primitive hunters made use of naturally occurring traps, such as holes in the ground and cliffs.*

## HUNTING WITH BOWS AND ARROWS AND TRAPS

Imagine a deserted land, an expanse of territory where as far as the eye can see there is not a single living, moving creature. Suddenly there is a herd of animals and a group of hunters, and the primeval exchange begins. The prize on offer is the survival of one species over another. The first hunters were nomads and often based their existence on one species of animal alone, following it in its continual wanderings from place to place. On any given day in the Paleolithic period there were confrontations between man and beast, but the outcome of these meetings was now already certain. The first big advance had already been made; the fight had become unequal. Man had developed the technical ability to make weapons, allowing early hunters to confront and beat

bigger animals. In the beginning their hunting weapons were of a light construction, being made of bone or horn; later they started making spears and bows and arrows.

The problems of transporting and preserving their catch, however, were often more difficult than catching it. A very large animal like an ox or bison had to be dismembered where it fell, and this could be a very risky operation because other animal species would try to take part in the banquet. To help solve this problem, hunters developed a network of caves which they used as shelter, giving them safety while they butchered their catch.

The low temperatures and biting winds taught early man, through trial and error, the benefits of extreme cold in preserving food, and so in this quite casual way began the story of frozen food and refrigeration.

axe

club

knife

spear point

The first tools primitive humans made were weapons for hunting and killing animals to procure the food necessary for their survival. The use of the bow and arrow permitted hunting from a distance, thus reducing the danger to the hunters.

bow and arrows with stone points

harpoon

harpoon

*Early fishermen used clubs and spears to catch fish while remaining on the banks of the water.*

## PRIMITIVE FISHING

Wind-swept prairies, arid and dry; chains of mountains, deserted and inaccessible; rivers, marshlands, and thousands of miles of coastland: This was Earth in prehistoric times.

There were also fishermen, who just like the hunters engaged in a continuous battle to affirm their dominance over the surrounding countryside and to take from it everything they might need to ensure their survival. The technical abilities people developed made them the winners in comparison with other animals around them.

Besides gathering shellfish and seaweed, prehistoric fishermen specialized in fishing techniques that allowed them to fully exploit that great and infinite larder: the sea. The biggest problem they faced was keeping themselves safe in the water. The dugout canoes and rush rafts were very unsafe, and it wasn't until Neolithic times and the introduction of oars that it became even half safe to venture farther afield with some degree of tranquility.

People who lived near lakes and rivers developed techniques that allowed them to catch bigger fish like pike, which appeared on the water's surface. Initially they used large clubs to beat the fish or spears to run them through. It wasn't long, however, before they began to utilize other equipment as well. The first hooks were made of thorns, which pierced the fish's mouth when it took the bait. Later they began to use hooks of bone and horn, which proved to be more flexible and resistant. Like hunters, fishermen saw a great change in their fishing methods with the introduction of the bow and arrow. Just like the hunters of the plateaus and plains, fishermen had a great many arrows at their disposal which they could launch at their prey from some distance away. Next they made harpoons, but what brought about the biggest change was the use of nets. Nets were made of sinew or little strips of plaited leather. They transformed fishing methods, turning fishing into a systematic activity that could feed entire settlements. Man's destiny was now determined; it was man who would rule the world, conquering first the land, then the seas and rivers.

*Later on, men fished from dugout canoes made from the trunks of trees and maneuvered by oars.*

## PRIMITIVE ANIMAL HUSBANDRY

Animals ran free on the plains and hills, still wild, never having had any rapport with man. When they came upon the first settle- ments, they brought ruin to whole fields of wild grains by eating the new shoots as soon as they appeared. This severely endangered the availability of food for the villagers. Something had to be done: guard the settle-

ments, chase the animals away, or keep them under control. This led to the raising and breeding of animals. A new rapport began to be established, no longer the usual battle between man and animal but a growing closeness between them. Animals became part of everyday life, as helpers and work mates.

The first animals to become domesticated and to be bred were goats and sheep, and later pigs as well. Pigs presented a problem in that they were not ruminants like sheep and goats and did not eat the grass and foliage that were readily available. Man decided to invest some food in this new venture—leftover meat scraps or grains and nuts from the woods. And so a new alliance

*Hunters took dried food with them on their hunts. Drying was one of the first food-preservation methods used by man.*

was born between man and animal.

An unforeseen effect of this primitive farming was that man, through the new-found closeness to sheep and goats, and especially cows, discovered a new food that was of enormous importance to future generations: milk and all the different ways of using and preserving it.

11

*Differences in diet led to differences in behavior: a diet based only on meat often caused aggressive behavior.*

*When people became farmers during the Neolithic period, their life became more sedentary: they still hunted, but returned to their village after each hunt.*

## THE NEOLITHIC REVOLUTION: TRIBES OF HUNTERS AND CLANS OF FARMERS

Slowly life on Earth began to change. The first isolated signs were insignificant. A settlement here, a small village there, some stones placed to form a circle in an attempt to define boundaries. From this time on, the land was not freely accessible to everyone. Human settlements began to lay claim to their own areas, placing signs and laying boundaries to delineate their own lands. The rearing of animals, together with the introduction of intensive sowing and reaping of crops and the development of new working tools and techniques, was a very long process and came to be known as the Neolithic revolution or era. During this period, which lasted for thousands of years, many primitive people continued to live their nomadic way of life.

The primitive nomads' diet was based almost entirely on the meat they were able to catch. Village dwellers, though, had discovered the benefits of working the land to give them better produce that was easier to obtain. This, by contrast, provided a diet based almost entirely on grains and beans, as well as the various foods that could be made from them.

# AGRICULTURE IN ANCIENT EGYPT

*Absolutely extraordinary.* This is what the tribesmen who were preparing to cultivate the Nile Valley in the Neolithic period must have thought when they realized that the river worked for them. In that part of the world nature was absolutely benign. When the reoccurring floodwaters of the Nile receded, they left behind a tract of rich, black, and fertile land. It was immediately obvious to the tribesmen that the land was ideal for cultivating wheat and barley. We know for certain that these were the first two grains familiar to the population of ancient Egypt, as their names were written in hieroglyphics, the most ancient form of writing. The oldest word was *barley* and was represented by three grains; then came *wheat*, represented by a single ear. We also know that ancient Egyptians later cultivated onions, garlic, lentils, beans, and vines because these words were found written in phonetics.

The population was so dependent on floodwaters that it became necessary to undertake a great deal of work, which when completed allowed people to control and

channel the waters more efficiently. Such was the gratitude of these people to their river that even today you can see these words written on a pyramid: *He who sees the Nile full will tremble. The fields laugh, the banks flood. The gifts of the gods come down from the sky. Man's face lights up, the gods' hearts are gladdened.*

A whole new civilization developed where wheat and barley grew in abundance, and in only a few centuries the population increased by one hundred. Just imagine that in the third century B.C. an Egyptian farmer could easily produce three times the amount of food required to feed his family. The excess usually went to feed the laborers involved in the massive works built by the Pharaohs; they still stand today as powerful representations of the ancient civilization of Egypt. Parallel to this increase in agricultural production were better environmental conditions, a new knowledge of working tools, and for the first tribes the problems of domesticating and rearing animals. Species like the ox, dog, goat, and especially the donkey were easily trained for work.

*The agriculture of ancient Egypt was based primarily on wheat and barley, which grew abundantly in the fertile soil along the Nile River.*

## AGRICULTURAL ORDER IN ROMAN TERRITORY

In Rome, peasants and slaves were men of peace while cultivating the land and tending their animals and men of war when called to battle to subdue other peoples and conquer new lands.

The life of an ancient Roman was ordered by centuries-old rules. Landowners were divided into five classes based on their wealth and had to contribute their men to form a regiment. The richest landowners were the first class, and their territories provided centuries of heavy infantry. The second and third classes were much lower on

the hierarchy. This is how land ownership led to supremacy in politics. Those who made the greatest contribution to the army by supplying men and arms gained supremacy in the government, along with the power to make political decisions. They elected the consuls and magistrates, made laws, and were even judges. All this led to the decline of the small farmers, constrained as they were by long years of military service, their numbers decimated by war, their fields impoverished by long absences. Thus began a social disintegration. The poorest people abandoned the land and moved to urban Rome, adding to the growing band of laborers and beggars.

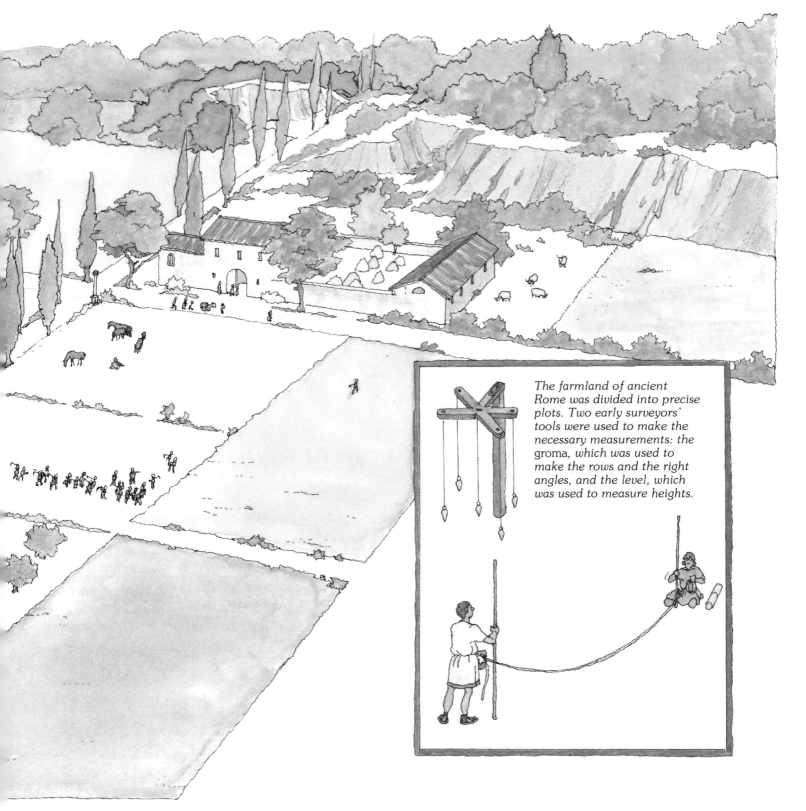

The farmland of ancient Rome was divided into precise plots. Two early surveyors' tools were used to make the necessary measurements: the groma, which was used to make the rows and the right angles, and the level, which was used to measure heights.

# THE ROMAN FARM

The city was finished, and all around it were extended areas of ordered and organized countryside that the Romans called *ager*, cultivated land. The farms were places full of life and work, where people organized the land in individual ways. Besides cultivated areas, there was the

*saltus*, wilderness—unproductive and inhospitable. The barbarians, who came from the north and did not cultivate the land, used these wild areas and woodlands to find

*The Roman farm represented the center of a complete production cycle in which raw materials were grown and transformed into food products.*

all the resources they needed, developing a woodcraft economy that was completely alien to the Romans, for whom the cultivation of wheat, vines, and olives took precedence over everything else. See how they plotted their farms, like perfect little microcosms. Cultivation took place outside the city walls, in the meadows, fields, vineyards, and kitchen gardens. Inside the city the produce was transformed into prepared food products like olive oil, wine, and bread. The Romans also ate much meat, and their farms certainly had cattle sheds and pens. They kept mostly sheep and goats because these could also supply milk, cheese, and wool.

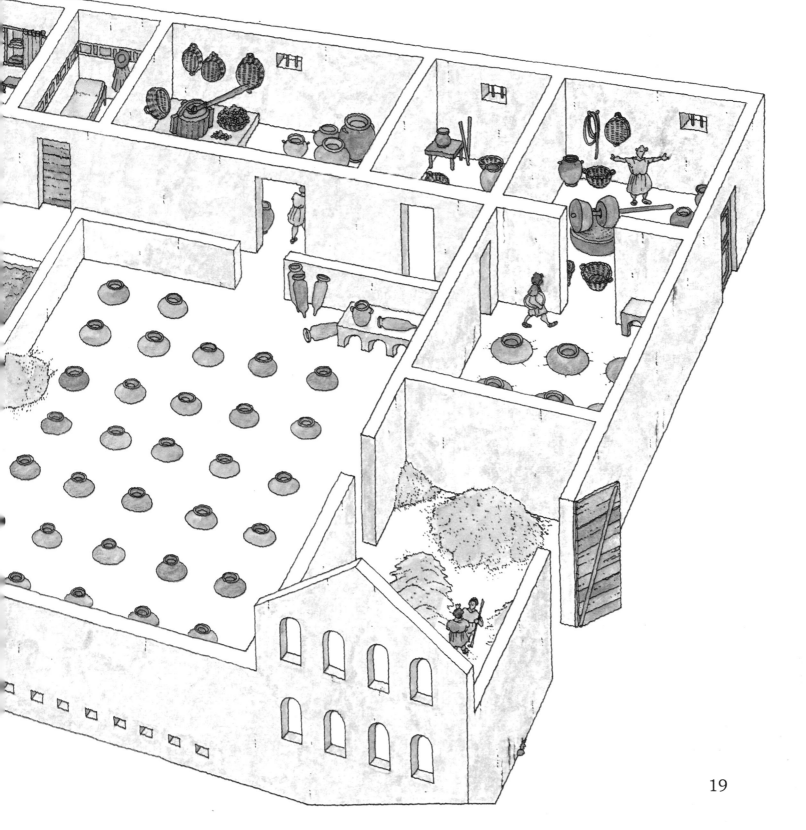

## MAKING BREAD

The earth was fruitful, putting its produce at man's disposal like gifts. But how did primitive people use these gifts, the wild grains that they came across? They realized that the edible part must be separated from the husk. They soon discovered that this was easier if the grain was first roasted. The edible grain was then ground with a mortar and pestle. The next important step was to add a little water, turning the rough flour into a semolina-type dough, which could already be called bread.

In ancient Egypt people discovered a new type of wheat, to which they added yeast. Dough made in this way could be left to rise before cooking, resulting in a lighter and tastier bread.

The increase in the consumption of bread went hand in hand with the development of new machinery and techniques for grinding grain. A new profession came to be established, that of the miller. The first milling process was achieved by manually pushing a rolling pin-shaped grinding wheel against a flat stone. The development of a new rotating grinding machine allowed people to use animals to provide a continuous motion, enabling the miller to produce flour in large quantities, which turned the miller's job into a very profitable activity.

As you see, the story of bread is deeply entwined with the story of man, of man's intelligence and growing technical expertise. The story of bread is also closely related to the history of the Christian religion, which in that century was beginning to establish itself in Rome. Bread was such an important symbol in Christianity that a thousand years later it was the reason or pretext for the schism between the empires of the east and west. The cause was a dispute over the host, whether it should be unleavened and without salt or made with yeast.

*The past and present sometimes blend and join. During excavations at Pompeii, the oven of a villa was found containing loaves of bread made in the same shape as the loaves many people still eat today.*

## TRANSPORTATION AND DISTRIBUTION: THE GRAIN SHIPS

On the sea's horizon is the outline of distant ships. Sometimes they are warships departing to conquer a new territory in the farthest province of the Roman Empire, and sometimes they are food ships carrying wheat and oil from the periphery of the Roman dominions. These are grain ships, and soon they will come in to dock and unload their precious cargoes, filling up the warehouses so that the distribution of free grain can begin. Dominance on the sea was essential for the Romans, not just for military reasons but also for commercial ones. Rome needed a lot of grain from Egypt, northern Africa, and Sicily. The proof of this was that when Carthage, the historic enemy of Rome, was razed to the ground, no one thought about destroying its precious reserves of grain. In fact, to ensure that they remained in control of the grain, Romans immediately subdued a seminomadic tribe from the inland.

*Ships sailed back and forth across the Mediterranean Sea bringing Rome the enormous quantities of grain needed to feed the imperial city's large population.*

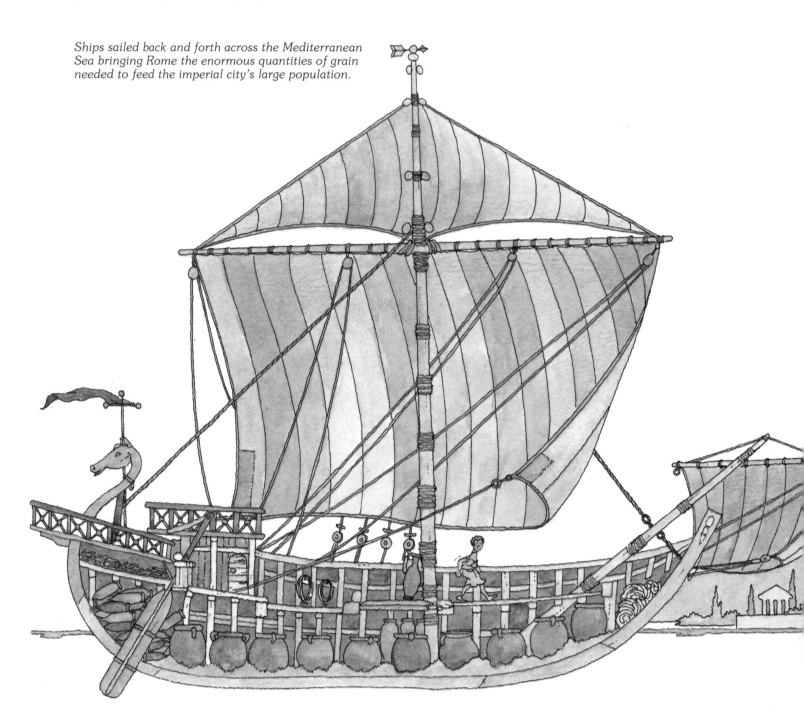

Just like the history of religion, the history of food is entwined with politics. The full warehouses most certainly contained a reserve that could be utilized when the crops failed and famine set in, but more than this they served politically by keeping up the supply of grain for free distribution by the authorities. In this way the imperial leaders of Rome tried to ensure the well-being of their citizens, especially the poorest and weakest. So important were the government's food distribution plans that they were surrounded by rigorous security measures. The ships carrying the grain were allowed to dock only at Ostia; offloading grain at any intermediate point resulted in severe punishment for the sailors involved: immediate deportation or even death. Once the grain arrived in port, it was checked and sorted, then loaded onto hundreds of barges, which slowly made their way up the Tiber until they finally reached Rome.

## A COVERED ROMAN MARKET

When the Romans needed to go shopping, they took a trip to a huge covered market. Once inside, they were immediately assailed by strong, spicy aromas. Between the stalls and stacked on the floor were sacks full of pepper, celery seeds, cumin, ginger, cinnamon, and many other exotic spices grown in lands far away from Rome and transported there for the rich people to buy. Also in the market were parsley, olives, raw beans, figs, and cheese. This is where most people stopped to buy, for the normal diet of most Romans consisted mainly of these products, accompanied by a cereal mixture, maybe *polenta*, made of millet or black bread. If, however, you were invited to dine with a rich neighbor, the food would be quite different. You would eat pike, which had been fished from, and only from, a special area of the Tiber. There would be *antipasti* (hors d'oeuvres) imported from Spain, ham from Gaul, oysters from Britain, roasted pig, and delicious wines. You would be well advised though to avoid *liquamen*, a brine sauce made by grinding together anchovies, mackerel, and salt and then left to ferment for many days in the hot sun. This sauce was also sold in the ancient markets of Rome.

*A day in the Roman market, where many kinds of food could be found, from delicacies for the most refined palate to the necessary foodstuffs for the common Roman family.*

## THE END OF THE CLASSICAL PERIOD

The Roman Empire began to dissolve, and new people began to come from far away, invading the country, attacking the cities, and bringing with them new habits and a new style of dress. They were called Goths, Vandals, and Franks, but they can all be referred to by one name: barbarians. They were meat eaters, and this gave them the energy, ability, and power to fight. They also drank a strange dense liquid made of fermented barley that later on, with the addition of hops, became the basis for beer.

The barbarians were completely different from the Romans in their tastes and habits, and their invasion led to the fall of imperial Rome. They started a time of chaos and poverty, and eventually a complete demographic collapse brought about a period of continuous famine, year after year. Cities were besieged and suffered continual battering at the hands of the barbarians. The countryside was the people's only hope.

Life in the country was not simple, but it was easier to procure food there than in the city. The rivers and lakes provided fish, and people could catch rabbits in the grasslands.

The forests and oak groves provided nuts and acorns with which to fatten the pigs, and growing wild in the fields were turnips, radishes, onions, cabbages, spinach, and many other edible plants. People were able to make bread with rye and wheat. Food was available, but it varied from region to region depending on the climate. The local economy was very uncertain. It didn't take much for hunger and famine to become

*The domestication of goats and sheep offered early humans two fundamental products for survival: milk for nutrition and wool for making warm clothing.*

established again. Some people set up abbeys with new orders of monks. These were places of refuge and protection with rigid rules; they provided an austere life of moderation far away from the excesses of the new invaders.

## NEW AGRICULTURAL TECHNIQUES OF THE MIDDLE AGES

People cultivated the land, and by their work, the decisions they made, and the tools they used they were able to make changes and create various agricultural landscapes. The farmer of the Middle Ages lived a life of great insecurity, constantly threatened by famine. The most pressing problem was how to increase the production of grains and get the best possible yield from the field. This was a time of great change. The water wheel, which became widespread, allowed farmers to use for the first time the free energy of the rivers. Where there was no running water, farmers developed the windmill, another source of energy that belonged to no one and was available to everyone.

Farmers soon learned that nature was not inexhaustible, and the intensive exploitation of their fields eventually had to be paid for with a gradual decrease in productivity. They discovered that nature must rest from time to time, untouched, if it is to give its best. They started to practice fallowing on some fields— two years of harvesting followed by one year of leaving the land untouched. This technique undoubtedly helped increase the land's productivity. Medieval man was not short of space in which to practice new farming techniques; in fact, all of Europe was rich in woodlands and prairies. What farmers really needed was a system that allowed them to exploit the land to their best advantage. One method was the plow; inherited from the

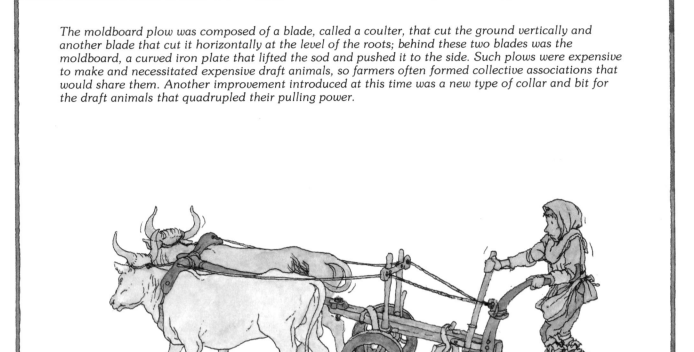

*The moldboard plow was composed of a blade, called a coulter, that cut the ground vertically and another blade that cut it horizontally at the level of the roots; behind these two blades was the moldboard, a curved iron plate that lifted the sod and pushed it to the side. Such plows were expensive to make and necessitated expensive draft animals, so farmers often formed collective associations that would share them. Another improvement introduced at this time was a new type of collar and bit for the draft animals that quadrupled their pulling power.*

*Mills gave people the ability to transform grains and other cereals into flour both quickly and inexpensively.*

Romans, it remained unchanged for centuries. Made of light wood, it dug a furrow in the earth. This simple implement often could not cope with uncultivated land, but farmers found a solution by inserting two wheels that served as a fulcrum for the plowman. This allowed him to exert more pressure on the plow, making it bite deeper into the earth. This deeper tilling resulted in better fertility.

This new tool also had repercussions on the raising of animals. A rivalry began between the horse and the ox; some farmers preferred the ox, solid and strong, and others preferred the much faster horse. The introduction of metal shoes that were nailed to the horse's hoofs finally won the battle for the horse, and it became the preferred animal in many parts of Europe.

*Before the discovery of America and the introduction of sugar from sugar cane, Europeans sweetened their food with honey from bees.*

## BEE KEEPING, SPICES, AND CURED MEATS

Sugar was another food that came from far away, the other side of the world. It became known in Europe only after the discovery of America, and sadly its story is linked to the dreadful exploitation of slaves on the sugar plantations of Brazil and the Caribbean. What did people use as a sweetener before sugar came to Europe? Honey, of course. The art of bee keeping was well known at that time.

European foods, and especially those that came from far away, like the spices from mysterious India, brought with them delicious aromas that evoked dreams of exotic places. Ostentatious, luxury foods gave a person social distinction, if only because of their price, which was beyond the range of ordinary people. That's why these foods were so highly prized. The Middle Ages and especially the Renaissance became known

as the "time of the spice madness." Menus were loaded with foods containing pepper, ginger, nutmeg, cinnamon, cloves, and mustards of various kinds. The doctors of the time who dealt with dietary matters encouraged the great popularity of spices, as they all believed that the "heat" from spices, and probably their strong flavors as well, aided digestion. During long periods of the year when fresh foods and meat were not available, the rich relied heavily on these luxury foods, and the peasants depended on dried or cured meats. They preserved food in salt, even though it was tiresome to grind down a lump of salt until it was fine enough for the salting process. They also preserved foods in brine, a solution of salt and water.

The first technique used to dry meat required that fresh meat be beaten to remove its liquid and then left exposed in the sun. People cured foods in an attempt to keep at bay the fear of poor harvests and famine.

30

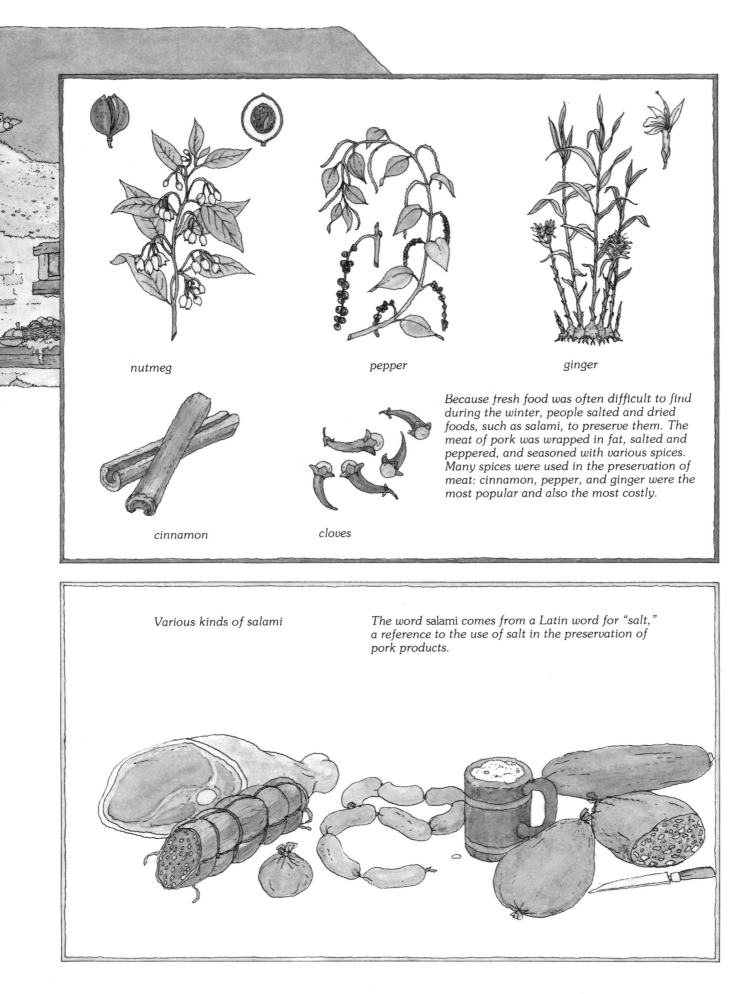

nutmeg

pepper

ginger

Because fresh food was often difficult to find during the winter, people salted and dried foods, such as salami, to preserve them. The meat of pork was wrapped in fat, salted and peppered, and seasoned with various spices. Many spices were used in the preservation of meat: cinnamon, pepper, and ginger were the most popular and also the most costly.

cinnamon

cloves

Various kinds of salami

The word salami comes from a Latin word for "salt," a reference to the use of salt in the preservation of pork products.

## THE FARMERS' VIEW OF THE RENAISSANCE

In the middle of the 1300s came the plague. Hundreds of thousands of people died all over Europe. After the scourge, life, as always, began anew, hope was rekindled, and everywhere a rapid increase in the population took place. New needs, new demands, and new necessities arose; the demand for food in particular led to a transformation in the agricultural landscape.

If the problem was that manuring the fields was not enough to increase fertility and production was poor, then the solution was always the same: just acquire some new land and start harvesting there. The Europe of the Renaissance was still heavily wooded, with many unexplored valleys. It was simply a question of broadening horizons. Farmers proceeded to cut down the forests, breaking up the earth and reclaiming the land.

This great necessity for food led to the

cultivation of new kinds of produce. Farmers started to grow maize, a new grain that Columbus had brought back from America. At first they grew it only in their gardens, but as more seeds became available they grew it in their fields. Another crop that did well and was widely grown was rice, which came to Italy from Spain.

Even after all this progress the world's economy was still uncertain, and farmers were unable to meet the demands made upon them. Years of poverty and famine set in again. But if you were hungry and there was no food, you could still dream of a place where abundance reigned. During this time there spread many wild stories about the land of milk and honey. These were written down, read, and told by word of mouth: the land of milk and honey, where giant saucepans of dumplings were served on mountains of cheese, where salmon hung on the doors of houses, and where grain fields were surrounded by fires on which roasted enormous pieces of meat.

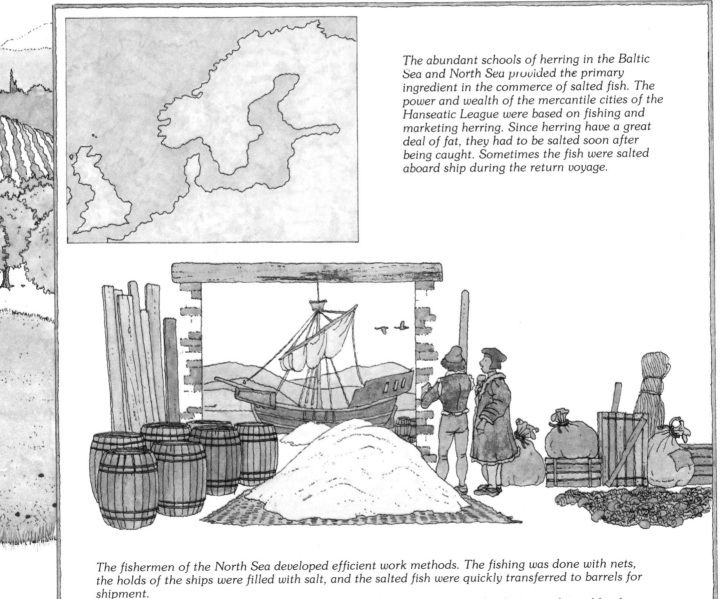

*The abundant schools of herring in the Baltic Sea and North Sea provided the primary ingredient in the commerce of salted fish. The power and wealth of the mercantile cities of the Hanseatic League were based on fishing and marketing herring. Since herring have a great deal of fat, they had to be salted soon after being caught. Sometimes the fish were salted aboard ship during the return voyage.*

*The fishermen of the North Sea developed efficient work methods. The fishing was done with nets, the holds of the ships were filled with salt, and the salted fish were quickly transferred to barrels for shipment.*
*Opposite: The growing need for land to cultivate led to an increase in the draining of marshland, deforestation, and the clearing of new land.*

*New foods arrived from the distant lands, offering new flavors and new ways of eating. But much time had to pass before these foods affected the diets of Europeans, for the eating habits of most Europeans were strongly tied to age-old traditions and uses, making them slow to accept new foods.*

maize

potatoes

tomatoes

strawberries

pepper

green beans

avocado

cacao

peanuts

pineapple

turkey

## ANIMALS AND VEGETABLES FROM THE NEW WORLD

Ships came from afar, from fabled and unknown places, trusting Columbus's routes, carried by the wind and the waves over the oceans. They were King Ferdinand and Queen Isabella's ships, and the sailors who came ashore had wonderful tales to tell of strange and mysterious places. They told of habits and lifestyles alien to the

Europeans, and the ships' holds were full of products people had never seen before. It was as though the sailors had been shopping on another planet. In fact, many of those foods were destined to change some of our most deep-rooted (eating and drinking) habits and to become an integral part of our diets.

Want a shopping list? The cases that were offloaded onto the quay contained cocoa and avocados, peanuts, pineapples, and strawberries. There were green beans, peppers, and chilies, tapioca and tomatoes. The latter were used only as ornamental plants. There were baskets containing something very precious—not gold or diamonds or spices from the Orient but seeds, maize seeds, and others that contained potatoes. Potatoes were completely unknown to Europeans, but once they were cultivated they became the staple diet of huge groups of the poorest country folk in Europe.

## THE RISKS OF MONOCULTURE: MAIZE AND POTATOES

Food to combat famine, the food of the poor; food of the countryside where nothing else is grown. Maize and potatoes shared the same fate. Both arrived from America, and they were both destined to become the staple diet for whole rural populations of Europe. Maize was cultivated because it was the main ingredient of polenta (cornmeal porridge, which can be eaten soft like mashed potatoes or oven-roasted or pan-fried in a more solid form).

Potatoes were chosen because they grew underground and thus were safe from the ravages of war and the trampling of horses' hoofs, which destroyed the fields and the harvests. Unfortunately, the outcome of monoculture was the opposite of what people expected. The earth needs to rest, and intensive monoculture depleted the soil, so the harvest grew ever poorer. Worse than this was the fact that a devastating new disease came with these foods: pellagra. It was brought on by a diet so lacking in essential vitamins that people weakened and succumbed to it. It caused insanity and death.

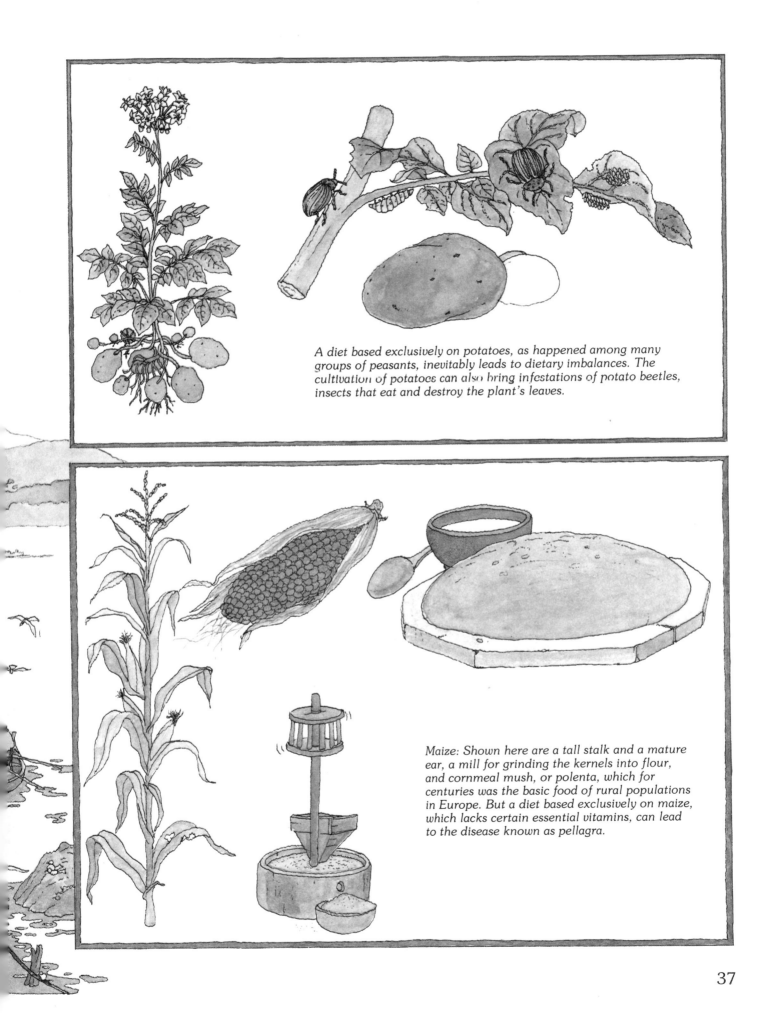

A diet based exclusively on potatoes, as happened among many groups of peasants, inevitably leads to dietary imbalances. The cultivation of potatoes can also bring infestations of potato beetles, insects that eat and destroy the plant's leaves.

Maize: Shown here are a tall stalk and a mature ear, a mill for grinding the kernels into flour, and cornmeal mush, or polenta, which for centuries was the basic food of rural populations in Europe. But a diet based exclusively on maize, which lacks certain essential vitamins, can lead to the disease known as pellagra.

## THE RATIONALIZATION OF CULTIVATION

As ancient man knew well, the earth is life, as well as being alive. People used to portray the earth as a huge drowsy animal. The earth cannot be exploited indiscriminately, because like everything else it must be allowed to rest and breathe. Just as you learn to know a new friend, ancient people learned about the earth by working with it and harvesting its bounty. They developed better cultivation practices and methods to protect and nurture their lands. This program of rationalization was an agricultural revolution, which increased productivity and guaranteed the quality of the produce. People abandoned the practice of deforestation and the exploitation of wild territories. They also stopped the practice of laying fallow their fields and introduced a new concept, crop rotation.

In a large portion of Europe, farmers adopted a four-year rotation system using wheat, rape, barley, and clover. Clover enriched the soil, and rape suffocated the weeds; both were used as animal feed. They discovered that growing vegetables made the land more fertile. They also used much more animal manure, which was more readily available now.

The English landowner Jethro Tull invented and advocated the use of a mechanical drill for sowing that saved seed.

The rationalization of agriculture led to an increase in productivity throughout Europe. The introduction of the first mechanical windmills, composed of a grindstone turned by wheels that are in turn moved by energy supplied by the wind, permitted the grinding into flour of increasing quantities of harvested grain.

## THE AMERICAN HARVESTERS

A barn, an enormous grain-filled barn, open to the sky. This is America in the 1800s, where huge expanses of land were available for cultivation but not enough laborers to work on them—in fact, just the reverse of conditions in most of Europe during the same period. The Americans had different problems to confront. They didn't need crop rotation or methods to preserve the land's fertility, for they had endless new land to break up, cultivate, and make productive. The prairies were immense, and to manage these huge areas American farmers needed machines. It is no wonder that during the 1800s many new machines were invented and patented.

There was McCormick's harvester, the mechanical thresher invented by Pitts in 1837, and the harvesters of Marsh and Appleby. The latter had a binder attachment to turn out baled hay. The huge combined harvesters were the biggest of all and required thirty horses to pull them.

There was a sort of technological frenzy during these years, a race to invent bigger, better machines, more able to exploit fully the riches on offer from the land. Harvesters were offloaded onto transcontinental trains that crisscrossed America after the end of the Civil War. Trains full of grains made their way to a port on the Atlantic coast, to be loaded onto the first steamship bound for Europe.

*Maple syrup is the concentrated sap of maple trees, which flows from the trees and is caught in buckets. Maple syrup is particularly popular in North America, where it is usually eaten on pancakes at breakfast.*

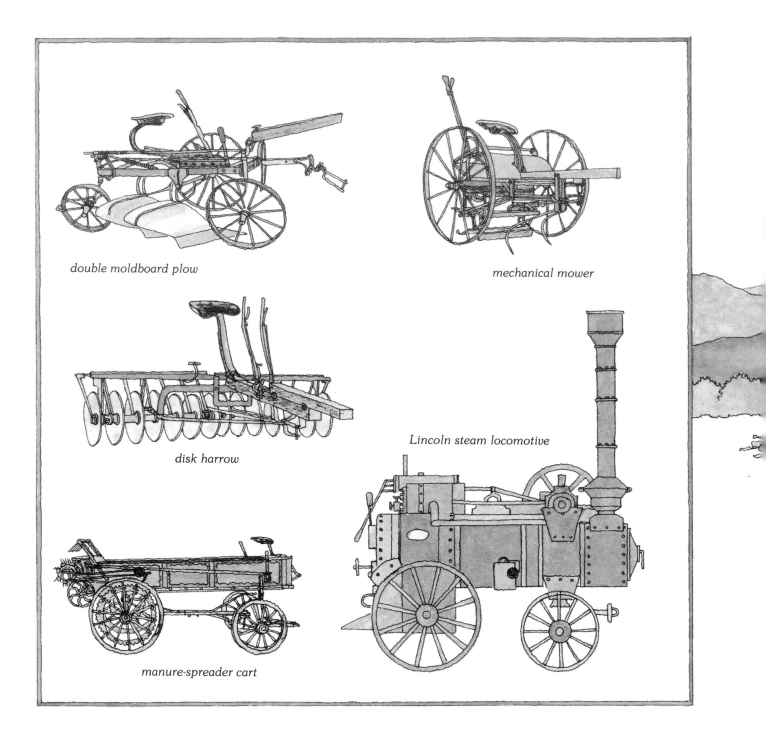

double moldboard plow

mechanical mower

disk harrow

Lincoln steam locomotive

manure-spreader cart

## STEAM ENGINES

Life in the country passes slowly and follows the rhythms of the seasons. The farmers' footsteps are slow, and their tasks are repetitious. Their work is silent in their fields, where silence has reigned since time began. Then one day there is a noise, and then a different noise—noises that nobody has ever heard before. It is a machine, strange and frightening: the very first steam-powered threshing and sowing machine, which shatters the silence all around it. The age of the machine has begun.

It was the beginning of the industrial revolution, which started in England and spread to the rest of Europe, that brought notable changes in everybody's lifestyle, rural and urban. The increase in the production of iron and cast iron meant that

the plow frame was made no longer of wood but of metal. Farmers began to make the plowshare (blade) of metal too, which made it a much more effective tool. The introduction of mechanization brought mixed results. On one hand the introduction of the threshing and sowing machine, invented by Jethro Tull, increased the yield of cereal crops and greatly reduced the amount of seed wasted during sowing. On the other hand these machines took over the jobs of the laborers who worked on the threshing floors. Peasants who relied on these jobs for their livelihood began to suffer unemployment.

"Change for the better" was the slogan of the enlightened landowners of England at the beginning of the 1800s. But the mechanization of agriculture didn't produce great results at first.

## FREEZING TECHNIQUES

The key word was *preservation*. It had always been one of people's dreams to be able to conserve food while it was plentiful, to see them through the bad harvests, and so to avoid famine, to actually live like in stories of the land of milk and honey, where food is always plentiful and available.

The process of preservation by freezing has been recorded since the Ice Age. In the eighth century B.C. the Chinese had discovered how to store winter ice to be used in the summer. They kept it in warehouses that stayed cold by evaporation. It wasn't until between 1830 and 1840 that the English patented an ice-making machine that worked by compressing ammonia, and from then on the old method of evaporation was abandoned. In 1877, they even held a banquet where for the first time ever the public could sample beef, fish, and poultry that had been frozen for six months. The success of refrigerators was immediate and enormous. Straightaway, factories were built for their mass production. The production of ice didn't mean just the ability to preserve food. It also meant

Water is put into metal molds that are moved across the length of the factory by a pulley system; along the way, the water solidifies, so that when the molds reach the far end and are turned over, the water has become blocks of ice that slide down to a collection point, where they are loaded on wagons and taken away.

the opening of new international food markets. Meat was imported from America and Argentina, where prairies are immense and can sustain huge herds of cattle. Europe's horizons were expanding. The world began to get a little smaller, and from then on the interdependence between the people of old Europe and the peoples of the New World across the ocean became ever greater.

The icebox is the ancestor of the modern refrigerator. Ice was first sold by traveling ice men, but eventually forms of iceboxes became common in homes.

# CANNED FOOD

Produce, preserve, and export. In the 1800s a new international market opened up and consequently the food industry was born. The question was how to transport food with the least deterioration and waste. The answer was to seal it inside metal cans, and so began the production of canned goods. Every story has its roots, and in this case it all started in France at the beginning of the nineteenth century with a man called Nicolas Appert. He had the idea of preserving fruit, vegetables, and meat inside glass bottles and then subjecting them to intense heat. Afterward he sealed the bottles carefully. The next decisive step was taken in England in 1812 by a man called Bryan Donkin, who replaced the glass container of Appert with one made of tin-plated iron, and from this evolved what we now call the tin can. In the beginning things were not as simple as they are today. People

had cans, but the can opener had not been invented yet, and early cans were very heavy and hard to open. Another problem was how to prevent the food inside the can from spoiling. People believed that this depended on emptying the can of air before sealing it, when in fact it was high temperatures that killed off the bacteria in the food.

This is where the stories of food and medicine merge. Toward the end of the century Louis Pasteur's theories on the role of microorganisms in fermentation and putrefaction processes became universally accepted. When these theories were applied to the food industry, canned goods became not just convenient but hygienically safe as well.

In the early days these cans were used only by soldiers and explorers, people who needed to carry around their food supply, but later on when cans became more advanced, they were mass-produced and available to everyone.

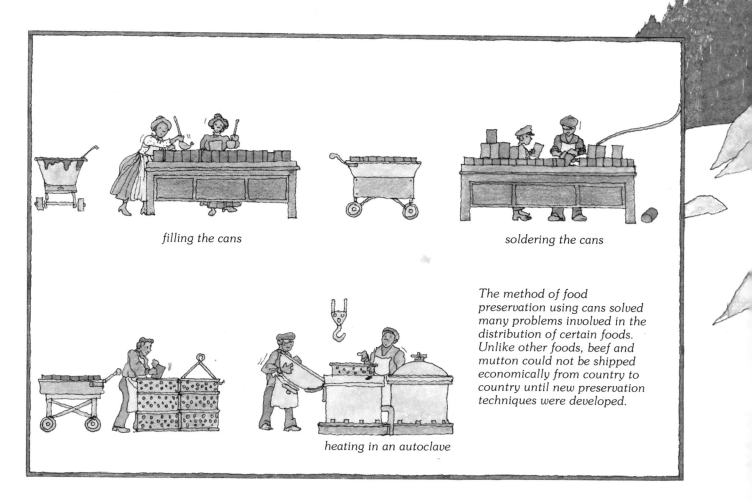

*filling the cans*

*soldering the cans*

*heating in an autoclave*

*The method of food preservation using cans solved many problems involved in the distribution of certain foods. Unlike other foods, beef and mutton could not be shipped economically from country to country until new preservation techniques were developed.*

The first can opener, invented by J. Webner in 1858, was hardly practical. The roller can opener introduced in 1925 was far more efficient.

## INTENSIVE FARMING

Big problems are showing up in our world. Large areas of Asia, Africa, and South America have populations that suffer from malnutrition, or at least substandard nutrition. The land is poor, yielding a miserable harvest. Rice and wheat, which are the staple foods of six out of ten people in these areas, are the crops that are affected the most. People have experimented by crossing various strains of plants in an attempt to produce varieties that are strong and disease resistant and that will produce an abundant harvest, even in geographically or climatically unfavorable places. This is a fascinating attempt but also potentially dangerous. The ecological system must be respected and kept in balance. The excessive use of fertilizers, fungicides, and parasiticides to increase productivity can lead to enormous ecological damage. Chemical insecticides like DDT have been banned in some countries, because once applied to the soil, they remain there, poisoning the land, air, and water.

*Aside from the use of fertilizers, fungicides, and pesticides, the practice of intensive agriculture includes the ancient method of terracing. Terracing demonstrates how humans, forever closely tied to the land and its products, have developed methods for farming every available space.*

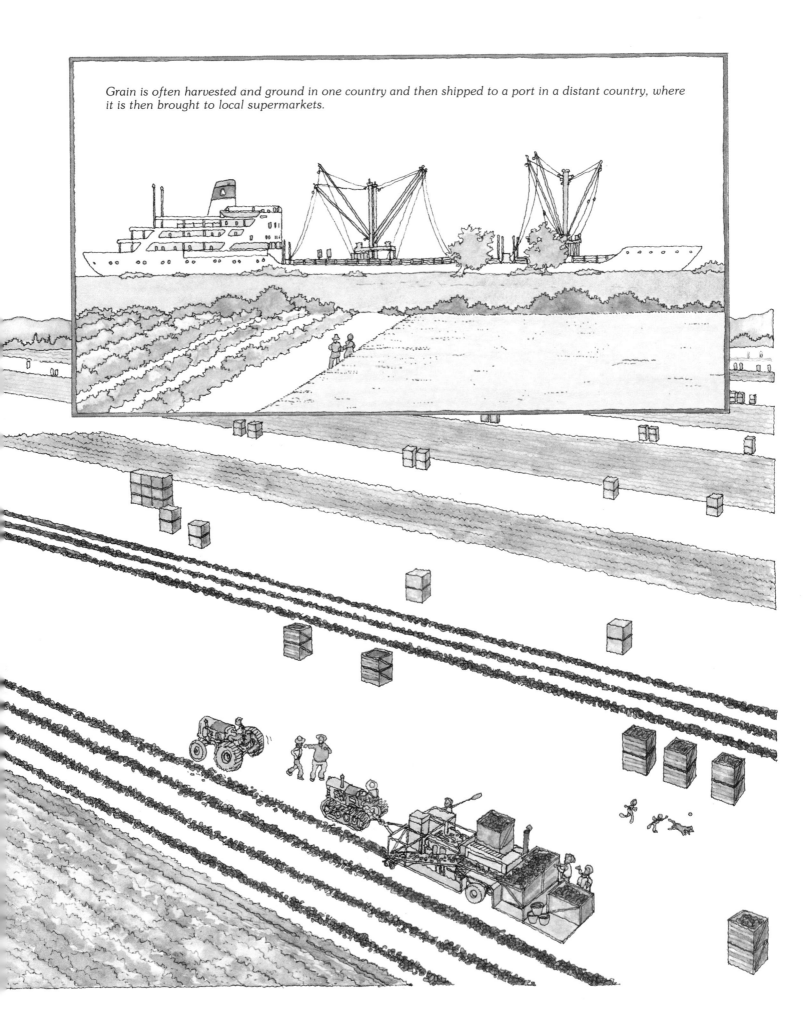

Grain is often harvested and ground in one country and then shipped to a port in a distant country, where it is then brought to local supermarkets.

*Humans have domesticated many animals and in doing so have brought about many changes in the animals themselves, as demonstrated by the pig, which began as the wild boar.*

*Hampshire breed*

*Duroc breed*

*Yorkshire breed*

## CATTLE RAISING AND BREED SELECTION

At the beginning of the 1800s, on the great plains of Texas, you could see drovers guiding great herds of longhorn cattle. Just a few short decades later the situation had changed radically: the Yankees had defeated the Native Americans, clearing the plains of the bison on which they depended, transforming them into huge, safe cattle pastures. New international markets created a great demand for food, especially meat. Steam engines revolutionized the transportation system, and trains allowed the movement of cattle from one place to another. Right up to the middle of the nineteenth century, cattle were transported live to the place where they were butchered. The long drives of the pretrain era tired the animals, reducing their weight and the quality of their meat.

The breeding of livestock led to enormous progress in terms of animal selection and crossbreeding, allowing animals to be bred specifically for the production of milk or meat. The result was an improvement in

*Domestic animals are kept in stalls and eat from troughs. This method of husbandry, known as closed housing, leads to increased meat on the animals because they move around very little.*

quantity and quality. During these years the numbers of cattle increased noticeably; newborn animals were healthier and fatter than the original Texan longhorns.

Parallel to the development of livestock was the introduction of a new social group, the great cattle rancher. In a short time he became very powerful, even to the point of influencing the decisions of the federal government.

*In the method of animal husbandry known as open housing, the animals are free to move about through fields or enormous fenced-in spaces and eat grass or feed supplied by machines.*

The studies and research of Louis Pasteur, the French chemist and biologist, inaugurated a new era in microbiology. Pasteur demonstrated that fermentation and infection are caused by germs present in the air, water, and ground. He discovered that the illnesses these germs brought can be prevented by injecting people with vaccines of live microorganisms.

*As soon as it is taken from cows, milk is moved in refrigerated containers to a dairy, where it is packed and delivered to stores.*

## FOOD SCIENCE: HYGIENE, PASTEURIZATION, AND STERILIZATION

A great farm with its fields full of cattle out to pasture: Here began the story of milk, a live food that must be treated in various ways to prevent the development of bacteria. After the milk was drawn from the cows (called milking), it was loaded directly onto large insulated tankers to ensure that the temperature remained low enough to prevent bacteria from developing. These tankers delivered the milk to the dairy.

Milk was used not only as a liquid food but also to make yogurt, butter, cheese, and so on. The techniques employed to make each product were quite different. Once the milk arrived at the plant, it was placed in huge insulated vats that were taken to the preparation areas where it was treated.

The most important methods for preserving milk were refrigeration and especially pasteurization and sterilization. The main problem was how to prevent the growth of bacteria in the milk. This was done by heating the milk to 67° C (145° F) for a few minutes (pasteurization) or bringing it to just over the boiling point (sterilization). In this way all microbes were eliminated. This is the kind of milk we find in our shops today—no longer a live food but a food you might call stilled by a process that has modified the milk's structure, changing its physical and chemical makeup.

# DIET

Eat only fruit and vegetables if you want to lose half a kilogram (just over a pound) a day, five kilograms (eleven pounds) a month. All around us people are talking about dieting and the best ways to lose weight. Dietetics is a science of our times. Dietitians play an important role in many people's lives. Industries have grown up around products specifically designed to help people lose weight. Serious studies have been made, and some people have set out simply to profit from this desire to lose weight. It's a question not just of beauty but also of good health. The rapport between us and our food is fun-

*Different activities and the number of calories consumed:*

sleep 65

sitting in a chair 100

reading aloud 105

sweeping 168

walking 200

walking quickly 300

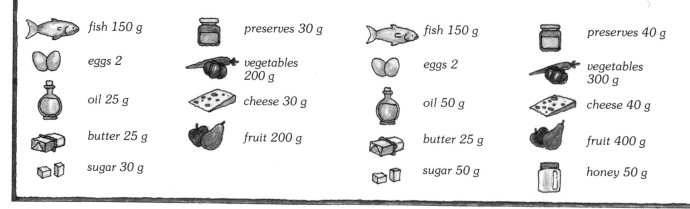

## ENERGY CONSUMPTION IN DIFFERENT PROFESSIONS AND SUITABLE DIETS

*Office worker: 2,600 calories*
*Because officer workers often spend many hours seated at a desk, their profession is sedentary and consumes limited energy.*
*A suitable diet might include 82 grams of fat, 387 grams of sugars, 90 grams of protein.*

fish 150 g
eggs 2
oil 25 g
butter 25 g
sugar 30 g

preserves 30 g
vegetables 200 g
cheese 30 g
fruit 200 g

*Tailor: 3,500 calories*
*From the point of view of energy consumption, a tailor is more active than an office worker, primarily because standing consumes more energy.*
*A suitable diet might include 105 grams of fat, 600 grams of sugars, 105 grams of protein.*

fish 150 g
eggs 2
oil 50 g
butter 25 g
sugar 50 g

preserves 40 g
vegetables 300 g
cheese 40 g
fruit 400 g
honey 50 g

damental. The problem is, what do we feed ourselves and what do our bodies actually need? Once eaten, food becomes energy, which provides us with the ability to move, work, play, and study. Everyone's needs differ—the young from the old, one profession from another. Each person needs a balanced diet to keep well and in good form.

Balance is the fundamental issue. Everything we do expends energy, and only through eating can we replace the energy we use. Each person arrives at this equilibrium by eating according to his or her own lifestyle. The sportsperson eats differently from the sedentary office worker, the young require more than the old—different needs for different reasons.

*standing 125*     *driving 133*     *typewriting 144*

*walking downstairs 365*     *swimming 430*     *walking upstairs 1,100*

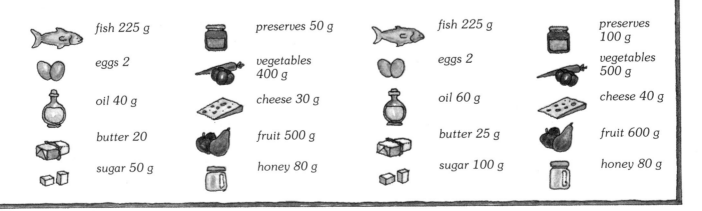

*Laborer: 4,130 calories*
*Road workers, masons, carpenters, farmers and all those who perform kinds of manual labor need more energy.*
*A suitable diet might include 125 grams of fat, 634 grams of sugars, 118 grams of protein*

| | | | |
|---|---|---|---|
| fish 225 g | | preserves 50 g | |
| eggs 2 | | vegetables 400 g | |
| oil 40 g | | cheese 30 g | |
| butter 20 | | fruit 500 g | |
| sugar 50 g | | honey 80 g | |

*Heavy laborer: 4,900 calories*
*Certain kinds of manual labor, such as moving furniture or operating a pneumatic drill, require even more energy.*
*A suitable diet might include 153 grams of fat, 751 grams of sugars, 133 grams of protein*

| | | | |
|---|---|---|---|
| fish 225 g | | preserves 100 g | |
| eggs 2 | | vegetables 500 g | |
| oil 60 g | | cheese 40 g | |
| butter 25 g | | fruit 600 g | |
| sugar 100 g | | honey 80 g | |

*Freeze-drying is a method of food preservation in which foods are vacuum sealed at a low temperature and dehydrated to remove all the liquid from them.*

*Another form of food preservation involves quick freezing; it is used both for fresh foods and precooked products.*

*Some foods can be concentrated by condensing or evaporating them, processes that remove two thirds of the water. Milk, for example, is available both concentrated and evaporated.*

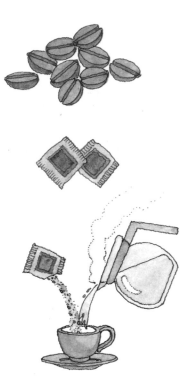

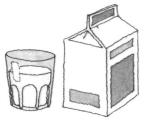

## NEW TECHNIQUES OF CONSERVATION

The arrival of the year 2000 makes everyone a little afraid and at the same time a little curious about the changes in our lives. We are talking about a leap into a new century, which must bring with it many new inventions. This date has been the subject of much speculation, which for the most part will be proved wrong or quite ridiculous. People used to say that by the year 2000 we will no longer bother to sit at the table to eat but simply take a pill, which will come in a variety of flavors and will be sufficient to nourish and satisfy our hunger for one whole day. But as we can see now, things have not turned out to be like that. Take a look at the foods on the supermarket shelves and see the new kinds of foods and the advances and changes that have been made in the last few

decades. There are freeze-dried and dried foods like soups, which require the addition of boiling water to make them edible. Think

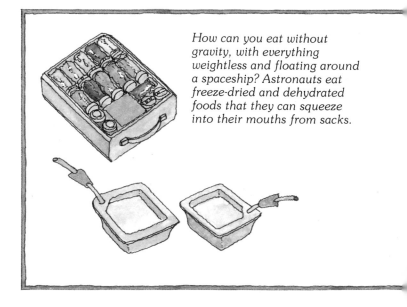

*How can you eat without gravity, with everything weightless and floating around a spaceship? Astronauts eat freeze-dried and dehydrated foods that they can squeeze into their mouths from sacks.*

how distant these vegetables are from those that are cultivated in the garden; think of the processes involved until they reach the plate.

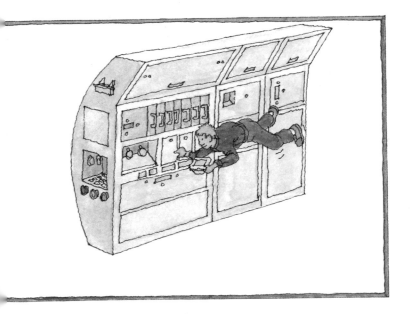

We have vacuum-packed foods, allowing them to be preserved longer. We can even buy machines to vacuum-pack food in our own homes. We can buy food that has been partly cooked and must finish cooking in our ovens. In most homes, then, you'll find not pills but good-quality food instead, still respected and enjoyed by everyone. Most of the time the foods we eat are of a better quality, with satisfaction guaranteed.

Has a change in our tastes brought about these changes? No, there is an underlying reason: a change in our life-styles. The pace of our lives is ever more hectic and growing more hurried by the day. Because we don't want to be defeated by this pace, we resort to the convenience of freeze-dried, precooked, and frozen foods, which appear to us as gifts that save us precious time, which we don't like to waste in unnecessary preparation.

# FACTORY SHIPS

There have always been ships, ships that plow through the seas with their holds like huge swollen bellies filled with food, which they carry from port to port, continent to continent. The first ships were the grain ships of the Romans, and then the ships of Columbus. There were also the ships of the European colonizers, which brought many new foods from the other side of the world. Last came the steamships, with their holds full of fish packed in ice. This was one of the first steps in the conservation of food—the technique of refrigeration. Refrigeration led to a major change in taste for large numbers of people. As fresh fish became available, people abandoned their traditional consumption of salted

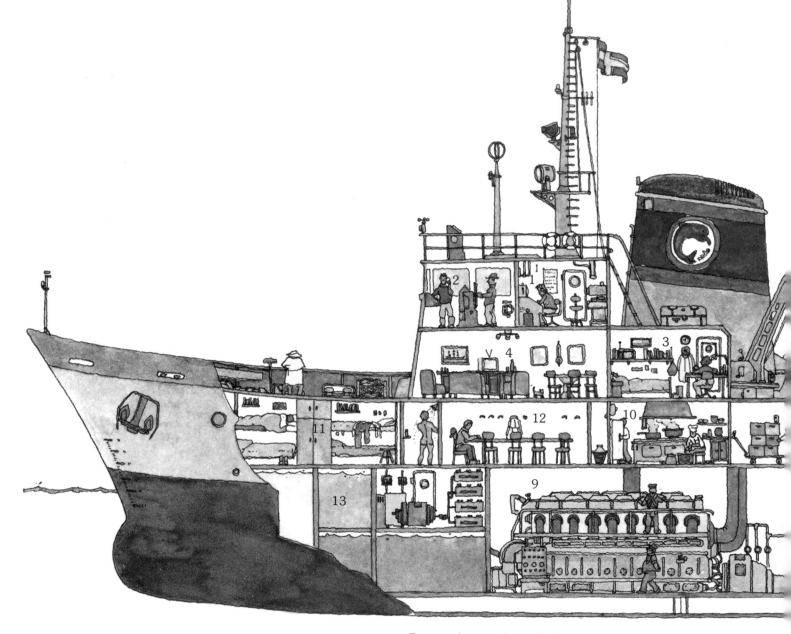

*Factory ships perform all the steps in the process of preparing fish that, up to a few decades ago, were done on land after the ship returned to port. The fish are cleaned, cut up, and stored in enormous refrigerated holds.*

herring, which was practically the only fish available to the poor people who lived in the cities at the beginning of the 1800s.

After the steamships came the factory ships, enormous floating industries. Their holds were set up for the complete production cycle. Fish from the depths of the cold sea came to the supermarket shelves and finally to our tables, ready to eat. Fish were caught, immediately frozen, and then packed into boxes.

Today, as in the past, the ships are met at the port by lorries, trains, airplanes, and goodness knows how many people who are involved in transporting goods from ports, until they finally reach our homes.

*This cutaway view of a factory ship shows: 1. radar room; 2. bridge; 3. captain's quarters; 4. recreation room; 5. net; 6. processing room; 7. assembly line; 8. refrigerated hold; 9. engine room; 10. galley; 11. bunks; 12. mess; 13. tanks.*

# NEW FOODS AND NEW PRODUCTS

At this point we can invent new names for the hypothetical foods we might be eating in the future. Some are already in use, for example, the tangelo, which doesn't exist in nature but is created by crossing tangerines with grapefruits. You can invent any number of new fruits, like the "orple" or "pearange," by crossing oranges with apples or oranges with pears. Worse still would be the "potatom," a cross between the potato and the tomato. These are just plays on words, but in reality this is the route scientists have chosen to guarantee the production of new vegetable and animal species that are disease resistant and appetizing and that satisfy people's growing desire for food in these last years of the century. Biology and the science of food help each other along—step by step they keep pace. They give rise to new words, studies, methods, and technologies, like cellular fusion, which allows the

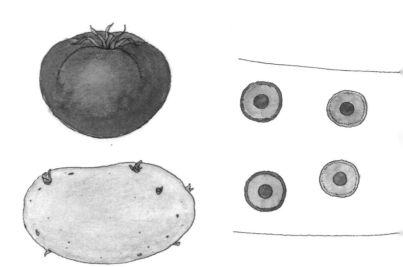

| a hybrid plant provides . . . | 1,000 seeds | after 6 generations over 3 years, a pure line is developed that gives . . . | 350 seeds | Plants and animals are bred to establish pure lines, which show little variation and have the best traits of the species. Pure lines offer the selection of desirable traits but very often involve a loss in terms of production. As with the natural products of the Earth, there is no guarantee that pure-line species will reproduce as well as the species from which they are derived. |
| a hybrid animal provides . . . | 200 eggs | after 9 generations over 9 years, a pure line is developed that produces . . . | 80 eggs | |
| a hybrid animal provides . . . | 14 piglets | after 9 generations over 18 years, a pure line is developed that produces . . . | a few piglets | |

60

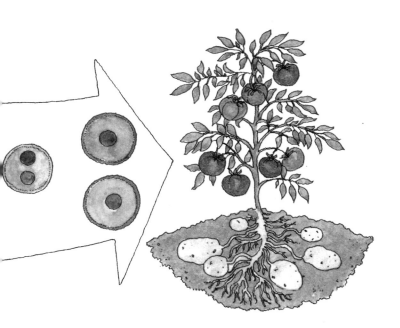

growth and development of fruit-bearing plants unheard of until today.

Very often you hear people speak of a future that is in fact already here and would more properly be named "the present." Proteins, carbohydrates, vitamins, and fats can all be reproduced in the laboratory, sometimes from the most unlikely materials. Proteins, for example, can be manufactured from soybeans and even combustible oil. The liquid waste from the refinement process of sugar beets is also used to make protein.

Suddenly new scenes unfold, remote possibilities like big laboratories—establishments that oversee the entire food-production cycle—become reality, serving millions of people.

A new road is being trodden, that of genetic engineering, fascinating but at the same time full of risks, the first of which is the belief that technology can fully supplant nature.

*Genetic engineering and the methods of cellular fusion have opened new frontiers and offered new possibilities; scientists are working on creating a new plant, which might be called* pomato, *that would produce tomatoes in its upper part and potatoes in the lower.*

*Hybridization, which can take place along two or four routes, is a technique that crosses different species or subspecies to obtain a hybrid species with the best traits of the original two, such as increased productivity or disease resistance.*

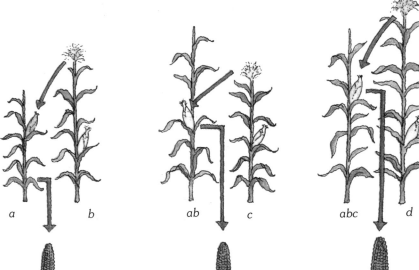

a    b         ab    c         abc    d

ab         abc         abcd

61

**Alemanni**. Germanic tribe that was living in the area of the Elbe River around 500 B.C. In the year 213 they tried to move into Roman territory but were defeated. When they later tried to expand into the area now known as France, they were defeated by the Franks under Clovis. The French word for German, *Allemand*, comes from their name.

**Animal husbandry**. The branch of agriculture concerned with the production and care of domestic animals, especially as a source of food, fuel, power, or raw materials.

**Annona**. In ancient Rome, the mythological personification of the year's food supplies. The word is thus also used for the quantities of grain and other foods distributed free each year to the citizens of Rome.

**Appleby binder and knotter**. Agricultural machine that harvests grain, gathers it, and ties it in sheaves.

**Barbarians**. The ancient Greeks and Romans called all uncivilized foreigners barbarians. The word was later used by the Romans for the various peoples living outside the borders of their empire and with the advent of Christianity, it was used for all non-Christians.

**Britannia**. The name given by the Romans to the portion of the island of Great Britain that they occupied. Julius Caesar invaded the island in 55 and 54 B.C., and it was conquered under the emperor Claudius in A.D. 43.

**Carthage**. Ancient city-state on the northern shore of Africa (near today's Tunisia). It was founded by the Phoenicians in the 9th century B.C. Carthage fought both the Greeks and the Romans and was finally destroyed by the Romans in 146 B.C.

**Civil War**. In U.S. history, the conflict (1861-65) between the Northern states and the Southern states that seceded from the Union and formed the Confederacy.

**Columbus, Christopher**. Navigator, famous as the discoverer of America, who was born in Genoa, Italy, in 1451 and died in Valladolid, Spain, in 1506. He left Palos, Spain, on August 3rd, 1492, and on October 12th he landed on a small island in the Bahama group, which he named San Salvador. He believed he had reached the Indies.

**Condensation**. The change of a substance from the gaseous (vapor) to the liquid state.

**DDT**. Abbreviation for *dichloro-diphenyl-trichloro-ethane*, an insecticide used to kill many kinds of insect. Because DDT is toxic to many animals, including humans, and harms the environment, its use has been banned in many countries.

**Dehydration**. Method of food preservation in which the liquid, usually water, is removed. Many foods can be dried or dehydrated for long-term preservation.

**Dietetics**. The branch of medicine that applies the principles of nutrition to the needs of humans at various stages of life and during disease in order to establish the best foods for an individual at a particular moment.

**Ferdinand II** or **Ferdinand the Catholic**. Spanish king (1452-1516). The son of John II of Aragon, Ferdinand united Spain by marrying Isabella of Castile in 1469.

**Franks**. Name for a group of Germanic tribes that fought against the Romans, the Suebi, the Vandals, and the Alans, and eventually settled in the region of Gaul, forming an empire that came to include most of today's France (which is named for the Franks).

**Freeze-drying.** Process in which food is dried in a frozen state for preservation.

**Frozen foods**. Products of the food preservation method of freezing; such foods are subjected to a quick-freezing process to maintain their taste, flavor, and appearance.

**Gaul**. Ancient name for the region of western Europe that today includes France. The Romans extended the name to include a portion of Italy, which they referred to as *Cisalpine Gaul* (Latin for "on this side of the Alps"); they called the portion of Gaul on the other side of the Alps *Transalpine Gaul*.

**Goths**. Germanic people, probably of Scandinavian origin, who spread from the Vistula River to the Black Sea, thus invading Roman provinces in Thrace, Moesia, Asia Minor, and Greece. When they reached the Black Sea (3rd century A.D.) the Goths divided into Visigoths (western Goths) and Ostrogoths (eastern Goths).

**Habitat**. The environment formed by a combination of certain climatic conditions and physical characteristics that permit certain species to establish themselves and reproduce.

**Hanseatic League**. Association of medieval German towns (Bremen, Lübeck, Hamburg) with common commercial goals. In German it was called the *Hansa*.

**Hybridization**. The crossing of two different species or different varieties of the same species to produce a hybrid. The process is often used in agriculture to produce plants with desirable qualities, such as greater strength or growth.

**Isabella I** or **Isabella the Catholic.** Queen of Spain (1451-1504). The queen of Castile, she united Spain when she married Ferdinand of Aragon in 1469. She is famous for the help she gave Christopher Columbus in his plan to reach the Indies.

**Liming**. The application to soil of calcium in various forms; lime benefits soil by neutralizing acids and improving texture. The value of liming was known to the ancient Romans.

**McCormick reaper**. Agricultural machine for harvesting grain, invented in the United States by Cyrus McCormick and his father, Robert. They sold their first reaper in 1840 and by 1871 had a factory capable of producing 10,000 machines per year.

**Marsh harvester**. Agricultural machine that harvests grain, invented in the United States in 1858 by Charles and William Wesley Marsh.

**Microbiology**. The branch of the science of biology that studies microscopic forms of life (such as algae, yeasts, bacteria, viruses).

**Neolithic**. Name for a prehistoric period characterized by the use of stone tools, the existence of settled villages, the domestication of plants and animals, and such crafts as pottery and weaving. It is also called the New Stone Age.

**Nile**. African river that is the longest river in the world, flowing 4,160 miles from Burundi in central Africa to its delta on the Mediterranean Sea near Cairo, Egypt.

**Paleolithic**. The earliest period of human development and the longest phase of human history; it includes the Pleistocene geologic epoch and spans the period from the appearance of the first prehistoric humans to the end of the last glacial period. It is also called the Old Stone Age.

**Pasteur, Louis**. French chemist (1822-95); one of the founders of modern bacteriology. He invented Pasteurization and developed vaccinations against anthrax and rabies.

**Pasteurization**. Method of partially sterilizing liquids; named for the French chemist Louis Pasteur, and used especially for milk, wine, and beer. The process destroys disease-causing organisms by heating the liquid and then rapidly cooling it.

**Pellagra**. Disease caused by a deficiency of niacin, which is found in milk, vegetables, and some cereals. The disease still exists in underdeveloped areas, particularly where the diet consists mainly of corn, which lacks niacin.

**Pillars of Hercules**. Ancient name for promontories flanking the entrance to the Strait of Gibraltar, which to the ancients marked the end of the Earth, beyond which was the unknown.

**Pitts mechanical thresher**. Agricultural machine for harvesting grain. John and Hiram Abial Pitts designed the first model in the United States in 1835.

**Potato beetle**. Name for a family of beetles destructive to the potato plant, in particular the Colorado potato beetle, which has black and yellow stripes and eats the leaves of potato plants.

**Prehistory**. Period of human history before writing and thus before written records. It is usually divided into periods—Paleolithic, Mesolithic, and Neolithic—and ages named for the tools used (stone, bronze, and iron).

**Quick-freezing**. Method of food preservation in which foods are frozen so rapidly that the ice crystals formed are too small to rupture the cells, thus the natural juices and flavor are preserved.

**Refrigeration**. Method of food preservation that involves drawing heat from a perishable substance to lower its temperature.

**Sterilization**. Process used to destroy the microorganisms in the atmosphere, in solids, and in liquids. Applied to food, sterilization permits long-term preservation.

**Tapioca**. Food product obtained from the fleshy root of the cassava. Because of its nutritional value it is particularly useful in the diets of children and the elderly.

**Terracing**. Method of preparing an area for cultivation that involves the creation of a series of terraces, or raised embankments with level tops, sometimes supported by walls.

**Tiber**. Third longest river in Italy after the Po and the Adige. It runs 251 miles from central Italy to the Tyrrhenian Sea.

**Tull, Jethro.** English agriculturist (1674-1741) and inventor of a mechanical drill for sowing seed. Tull studied law at Oxford and designed the machine while helping his father run the family estate. The laborers on the estate went on strike, fearing the machine would take away their work.

**Vandals**. Name originally applied to the inhabitants of the coast of the Baltic Sea. Under pressure from other tribes and suffering difficult economic conditions, they migrated to Rhaetia, where they made peace with the Roman Empire. In 455 the Vandals attacked Rome, sacking and partially destroying the city. Their rule lasted until 533, when they were defeated by a Roman army under Belisarius.

**Yankee**. Term originally used for a native of New England that during the Civil War came to be applied to all inhabitants of the northern United States.

HOUSES

CLOTHING

COMMUNICATION

FOOD

TRANSPORTATION

TECHNOLOGY